Elusive Moose

For my friend, Lois — C. B.

For my daughter Lesley, who inspired my
continued search for the elusive moose — J. G.

With special thanks from the author to Irmelin Sandman Lilius,
for her grace and wealth of moose lore, Dr. Ilpo K. Hanski,
Senior Curator at the Zoological Museum, Helsinki, Finland and
Dr. Vesa Ruusila at the Finnish Game and Fisheries Institute.

Barefoot Books
2067 Massachusetts Ave
Cambridge, MA 02140

This book has been printed on 100% acid-free paper
Graphic design by Judy Linard, London. Color separation by Grafiscan, Verona
Printed and bound in China by PrintPlus Ltd

This book was typeset in 22 on 29 point Plantin Schoolbook Bold
The illustrations were prepared in antique fabrics and felt with sequins, buttons,
beads and assorted bric-a-brac

Library of Congress Cataloging-in-Publication Data
Gannij, Joan.
        Elusive moose / Joan Gannij, Clare Beaton.
        p. cm.
        ISBN 1-905236-75-1
                1. Moose--Juvenile literature. I. Beaton, Clare. II. Title.
        QL737.U55G36 2006
        590--dc22

                                                                        2005030374

                                1 3 5 7 9 8 6 4 2

Elusive Moose

Written by Joan Gannij

Illustrated by Clare Beaton

Barefoot Books
Celebrating Art and Story

Far off in the north
I've seen horses with foals.

I've spied beaver families
And marmots and moles.

I've met geese and goslings;
I've crept very near.

I've seen a brown bear,
I've seen caribou deer.

At night I've heard badgers
And green frogs that leap.

But I dream about moose
As I slumber and sleep.

I've spotted fish eagles
And cranes in the sky.

I've even seen grouse;
I've seen squirrels that fly!

But where are the moose
When the autumn leaves fall?

Where are they hiding?
They're so big and tall!

I've tracked down moose hoof prints
On land white with snow.

I've seen Arctic foxes
And hares come and go.

But moose are elusive.
Moose roam where they please.

I wish I could see one
Just once. May I, please?

Animals of the Northern Lands

Arctic foxes are gray-blue in summer and light gray or white in winter. They feed on fish, birds, small mammals and berries.

Badgers have short legs, a flat body and a silver-gray tail. They live in underground dens lined with leaves and grass.

Beavers are agile and powerful, and they are superb dam builders. Their front teeth are so strong that they are able to fell a tree in less than five minutes!

Brown bears (sometimes called "grizzly bears" in North America) often live alone and like to eat grass, bulbs, roots and berries as well as insects and especially fish (salmon).

Caribou deer feed on plants, nuts and corn, as well as trees and twigs. They are good swimmers and runners. In the summer they are reddish-brown and they turn to a more neutral grayish-brown in the winter.

Cranes are large, elegant and graceful birds that dwell in wetlands and grasslands. The crane in this book is a sandhill crane.

Fish eagles live only in North America, usually near large lakes. They have a wing span of up to 8 feet (240 cm).

Flying squirrels live entirely in trees. They have a fold of skin stretching from the wrist of each front leg to the ankle of each rear leg, so that they can glide from tree to tree.

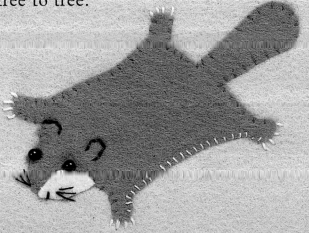

Frogs are ancient creatures, with ancestors going back 190 million years. Wherever there is fresh water, there are likely to be frogs! The only continent where they are not found is Antarctica.

Grouse are small birds with brown speckled feathers that serve as camouflage. They like to nest close to the ground in high, exposed places.

Horses that live in the wild, like the graceful ones found in Iceland, are a little smaller than normal horses, but are not ponies. They have a strong sense of direction and a lot of stamina, so in the past they were an essential form of transportation.

Marmots are large ground-dwelling squirrels that are often seen on mountains in the summer months. They hibernate from September until May. The groundhog is a kind of marmot.

Moles spend most of their time in underground burrows. They have short, powerful, hand-shaped front legs to help them move soil.

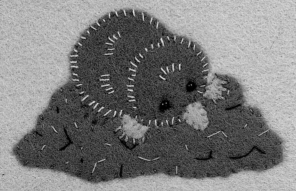

Snow geese can be white with black tail feathers like the ones in this book, or white-headed with a blue-gray body. They fly in long lines or V-shaped formations when they migrate for the winter to the Arctic region.

Snowshoe hares can only be found in North America. They are shy and secretive, and take their name from their big, furry feet, which have four long toes, allowing them to move easily over snow.

Animal Tracks

Redpoll Finch

Here are the tracks of the animals you can
see in the winter scenes of this book:

Arctic Fox

Moose

Snowshoe Hare

Guess who?

Meet the Moose!

The moose is the largest member of the deer family in the world. Moose live in wooded areas of Canada and the northern United States (Alaska, Maine), and in Nordic countries like Finland and Norway. There are also a few moose in Russia. Moose are shy animals and they like to live alone.

During the warmer months, moose spend their time near lakes and marshes. When winter comes, they move to forested areas. In warmer months, they eat water plants. They also feed on the branches and leaves of willow, birch and aspen trees. In fall, they eat shrubs and berries, and in winter they survive on twigs, berries and branches.

Moose have large ears, a wide droopy nose and an overhanging top lip. A long flap of fur-covered skin called a bell dangles under their chins. They have poor eyesight and rely on their keen sense of smell and hearing. They often stop and listen while eating.

Moose vary in color from almost black to light brown, becoming grayish in winter. Male moose have large, wide antlers that they shed every year after the fall mating season. The antlers grow back in the early spring, usually larger than before. A rack of antlers can range from 4–5 feet (120–150 cm) across. The Alaskan moose have the largest antlers — more than 6 feet (2 meters) wide!

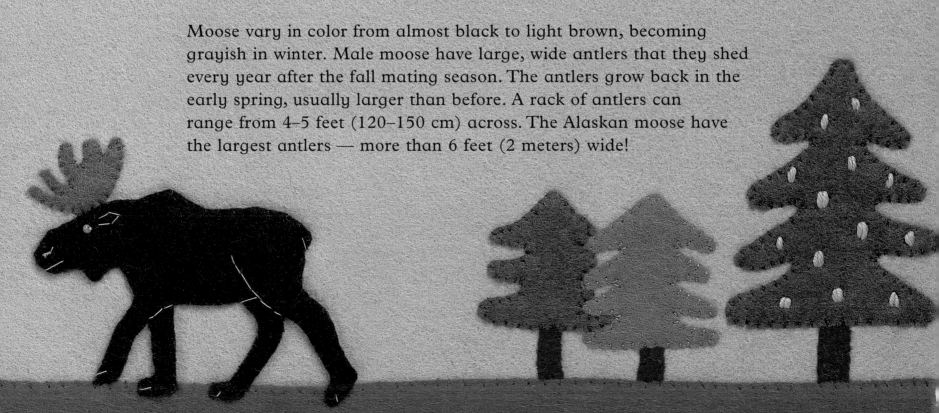

Barefoot Books
Celebrating Art and Story

At Barefoot Books, we celebrate art and story that opens
the hearts and minds of children from all walks of life, inspiring
them to read deeper, search further, and explore their own creative gifts.
Taking our inspiration from many different cultures, we focus on themes that
encourage independence of spirit, enthusiasm for learning, and sharing of
the world's diversity. Interactive, playful and beautiful, our products
combine the best of the present with the best of the past to
educate our children as the caretakers of tomorrow.

www.barefootbooks.com